Juliet
the Valentine
Fairy

Special thanks
to Kristin Earhart

ORCHARD BOOKS
338 Euston Road, London NW1 3BH
Orchard Books Australia
Level 17/207 Kent Street, Sydney, NSW 2000

A Paperback Original
First published in the UK in 2010 by Orchard Books

HiT entertainment

A CIP catalogue record for this book is available
from the British Library.

ISBN 978 1 40831 135 6

1 3 5 7 9 10 8 6 4 2

Printed in Great Britain

The paper and board used in this paperback are natural recyclable
products made from wood grown in sustainable forests. The
manufacturing processes conform to the environmental regulations
of the country of origin.

Orchard Books is a division of Hachette Children's Books,
an Hachette UK company

www.hachette.co.uk

Juliet
the Valentine
Fairy

by Daisy Meadows

ORCHARD BOOKS

www.rainbowmagic.co.uk

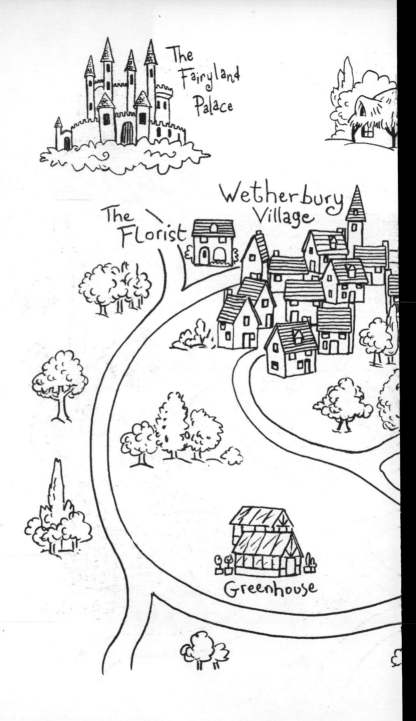

The Fairyland Palace

The Florist

Wetherbury Village

Greenhouse

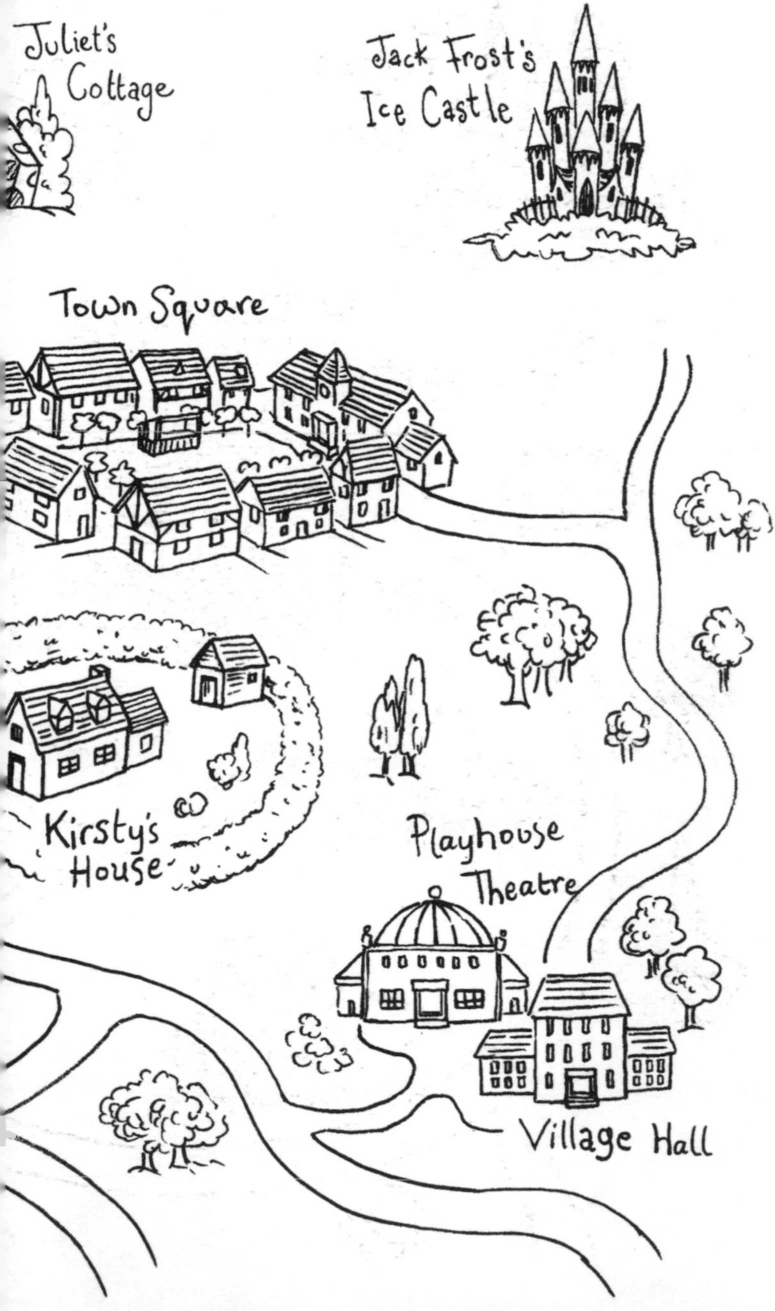

Juliet's Cottage

Jack Frost's Ice Castle

Town Square

Kirsty's House

Playhouse Theatre

Village Hall

It's Valentine's Day and love is everywhere,
but I, Jack Frost, feel it isn't fair.
Friends and families and sweethearts, too,
I've got a mean surprise for you.

This day is no longer nice.
If you celebrate, you will pay the price.
Giving cards and gifts is a big mistake,
These things will cause your hearts to break.

Card-making Mishap

Contents

A Weekend Guest

Kirsty Tate paced from the front hall
to the kitchen and back again. Pulling
aside the curtain, she looked out of the
window. There was still no sign of her best
friend, Rachel Walker. Kirsty glanced at
the grandfather clock in the corner. The
Valentine's Workshop would have already
started. She hoped her friend wouldn't be

 much longer or they would miss it.

Anxiously, Kirsty stared out of the window, hoping the Walkers' car would magically appear – but she knew that she couldn't just make it happen. The truth was, she and Rachel knew a lot about magic! They had learned about it from their friends, the Rainbow Magic fairies.

The two girls had first met on a trip to Rainspell Island when they had helped the seven Rainbow Fairies, who had been sent away from Fairyland by wicked Jack Frost. The king and queen of Fairyland had come to rely on the girls whenever Jack Frost and his goblins were causing trouble.

Kirsty felt happy thinking about her fairy friends, and even happier when she saw Rachel's car turning into their road.

As it pulled into the Tates' driveway, Rachel waved cheerfully to Kirsty, who hurried out to help with her friend's bag.

"You must come in for a cup of tea." Kirsty's mum had appeared at the door to speak to Rachel's mother.

"I'd love to," smiled Mrs Walker.

"I'm so glad you're here," Kirsty said, hugging her best friend. "I was starting to worry. We'll just put your bag in my

room and go straight to the Village Hall."

"But I thought the Valentine's Workshop was this evening," Rachel said, looking confused.

"No, it's already started," Kirsty replied. "But we should still have time to make some great Valentine's things," she added with a smile. "Come on, let's tell my dad we're ready to go."

The two friends dropped Rachel's bag upstairs and headed to the kitchen.

Through the window over the sink, they could see Kirsty's father working in the back garden. Kirsty poked her head out of the back door.

"Dad, can you take us to the Village Hall now?" she asked. "Rachel's here."

Mr Tate looked up from a pile of wood and chicken wire. "Hi, Rachel!" he called. Then he wiped his forehead with his sleeve and looked at Kirsty. "I completely forgot that I was supposed to take you girls to the workshop. It's such nice weather today, I started making the new compost bin for your mum." He glanced down at the pile of building materials and his brow creased. "I still have a lot to do, and I've made a bit of a mess. Do you think you girls could cycle over to the Village Hall?"

"Of course," Kirsty smiled. "And it is very nice out after all," she said, looking up at the blue sky.

"I'll pick you up afterwards. We can put the bikes in the boot," Mr Tate said.

"Thanks, Dad – the workshop finishes at 6.30," replied Kirsty. "See you then!"

Mr Tate gave his daughter a warm smile and watched as she grabbed her friend's hand and ran back inside the house.

"Bye, Mum," Rachel put her head round the sitting-room door.

"Bye, sweetheart," said Mrs Walker. "Give me a call and let me know what time I should pick you up on Sunday."

Rachel gave her a hug and then hurried outside after her friend.

"You can ride my new bike," Kirsty

offered as they ran down the garden path, pointing to a purple bike with a basket on the front.

Kirsty grabbed her old blue bike and once Rachel was on the old one, they set off.

"This bike was my cousin's once upon a time. It's a little small, but I can still ride it," Kirsty grinned. "And I bet I can beat you there!"

"You're on!" laughed Rachel.

Valentine's Workshop

After the quick ride into Wetherbury Village, Kirsty and Rachel turned off the road and into the Village Hall car park.

"What a lovely building," Rachel said, climbing off her bike.

"Our workshop is on the third floor," Kirsty smiled, turning the key on her bike lock.

The girls ran up the stairs to the classroom. A tall man with a beard greeted them. "Hello, Kirsty," he said. "And you must be Rachel." The man smiled as he marked their names on his clipboard. "Hello, Mr Brown," Kirsty said. "I'm sorry we're late."

Mr Brown shook his head. "Don't worry, my dear. All the art supplies are out on the tables," he said. "You still have plenty of time to make something from the heart."

Kirsty and Rachel looked at each other, trying not to giggle.

"Come on," Kirsty said, walking over to a table with two spare seats and picking out some paper and pens. "Let's get started. I want to make my parents a really special card."

"That's a lovely idea," said Rachel.

At the next table, two friends began arguing loudly. "You're copying me," declared a girl with long brown plaits.

"I was using the star stickers first!" the other girl replied.

"No, you weren't." The two girls scowled at each other until one pushed her chair back loudly and stood up. "Fine, I'm changing tables," she huffed, heading off to find a new seat.

Almost immediately, Kirsty and Rachel heard another disagreement coming from a different table. "Stop kicking me!" A boy's voice carried across the room.

"Tom? Andrew? What seems to be the problem?" Mr Brown asked.

Kirsty glanced over and saw two boys from her school giving each other icy glares. "They're best friends," Kirsty whispered to Rachel in shock. "They never fight."

The girls looked at each other with

raised eyebrows. "Do you think something funny is going on?" Rachel asked.

"It certainly seems that way," Kirsty answered.

"You're right!" a tiny voice sang out so

quietly that only Rachel and Kirsty could hear.

"What?" Rachel and Kirsty both said, each glancing at each other with surprised expressions on their faces.

"You're right," the small, sweet voice said again. "Something funny *is* going on." After a pause, the voice became serious. "Well, actually, it's not funny at all."

The two girls peered around the room until their eyes came to rest upon a fairy!

She was so small that she was hiding in a glass jar of glitter, right in front of them on the table.

"Oh, hello!" Rachel gasped. Kirsty immediately folded a large piece of card and propped it up on the table, so no one else could see their fairy friend.

As soon as the coast was clear, the fairy fluttered out of the jar. She unfolded her wings, and magical hearts swirled around her. Her long brown hair fell in waves past her shoulders, and she wore a pink jumper and a denim skirt with two hearts stitched to the front. Her beaded necklace had a red heart pendant on it.

But more than anything, Kirsty and Rachel noticed the pretty fairy's big brown eyes – which were on the verge of tears.

Juliet's Story

"Kirsty and Rachel," the fairy said, sighing. "I'm so lucky I found you! It's the only good thing that's happened all day." A single tear ran down one of her rosy cheeks.

Kirsty and Rachel looked at the little fairy with concern.

"Oh, please forgive me," the fairy said, perking up a little. "I know your names, but you don't know mine!" She brushed the extra sparkles from her skirt and bent her knees in a little curtsy. "I'm Juliet the Valentine Fairy. It's my job to make sure that Valentine's Day is full of love and happiness, both in Fairyland and the human world. But I'm afraid I've messed everything up this year!"

"Oh, Juliet. I'm sure it's not that bad," Rachel said, trying to reassure the fairy.

"Oh, but it is," Juliet said sadly. "You see, friends and families are fighting everywhere. Sweethearts are falling out of love. People are not thinking about one another's feelings." She pulled out a pink tissue and sniffed. "Everything that makes Valentine's Day special is coming apart!" She buried her face in her hands.

"Tell us what happened," Kirsty suggested. "Maybe we can help."

Juliet raised her head. "I was just finishing making this year's Valentine's objects – a card and two presents – when I heard some beautiful music. I went outside to see where it was coming from, but no one was there. When I went back into my cottage, I realised that the objects for Valentine's Day had gone!" The fairy's shoulders slumped. "I grabbed my wand and raced outside just in time to see three

goblins running down the lane! I tried
to stop them, but I couldn't cast a spell
because my fingers were still too sticky
from the glue I'd been using. As soon
as I got a good grip on my wand, the
spell came tumbling out. But just at that
moment, Jack Frost appeared and
cast a spell that rocketed straight back
and stopped my spell." Juliet twirled her
hands around.

"Now the Valentine's objects are lost somewhere in the human world. If I don't find them and return them to Fairyland, Valentine's Day won't be the same."

"What happens if you don't get the objects back?" Rachel asked.

"Jack Frost's spell will ensure that every card or present will have the opposite effect that it should," Juliet said, shaking her head sadly. "And this time, he's given the goblins a wand that can mix up messages. They're using it to change the meanings of cards, notes and emails. It's a mess!"

Kirsty and Rachel felt their hearts sink.

They had already seen what could happen by the goings-on in their Valentine's Workshop!

"The three missing objects stand for three kinds of love," Juliet explained to the girls. "First, there's the Valentine's card which represents family love. Second," the fairy said, "there's the red rose. It stands for sweetheart love. And finally, there's the box of chocolate hearts. Those are for friendship. Each object is tied with a sparkly red ribbon."

The girls thought about the special kinds of love. They couldn't let them be ruined!

"We have to do something!" declared Rachel.

"I would love your help," Juliet replied, giving the girls a tiny smile. "But, for now, let's just be on the lookout. Jack Frost told his goblins to do whatever they had to do so that we wouldn't get the magical presents and card back."

Kirsty nodded, remembering how Fairyland magic worked. The presents and card needed to be back in Fairyland before the day would be magical again!

"I suppose you girls should just work on your Valentine's cards for now," Juliet said, shrugging. "At least until we find a clue...or until the goblins find us."

No-good Goblins

Kirsty took Juliet's advice and immediately went back to making her Valentine's card. If there was nothing they could do at the moment, that should at least take their minds off it. She reached in front of Rachel for some pipe cleaners and tissue paper.

"Why are you bothering with that silly card?" Rachel asked. "If we don't hurry up and find Juliet's card and presents, it won't matter if you finish it or not—" Rachel stopped herself and put her hand over her mouth. "I'm sorry, Kirsty." She dropped her eyes to the floor. "I don't know what came over me. It just came out."

"Don't worry, Rachel," said Kirsty. "It's just Jack Frost's horrid magic working. If he can get between *us*, just think what horrible things he must be doing to other people!"

"It's true, girls," said Juliet. "We mustn't argue."

Kirsty and Rachel both looked down in embarrassment.

"I'd like some more decorations," Kirsty suddenly announced, studying her Valentine's card. She stood up and walked over to Mr Brown's desk.

Immediately, Juliet flitted to Rachel's shoulder and hid behind her hair. "Let's go with her," whispered the fairy. "It's best to stick together."

Rachel nodded and quickly stood up.

"Why, Kirsty," Mr Brown said, "your card is lovely."

"Thank you," replied Kirsty, looking at the work she'd done so far. The front had delicate tissue-paper flowers clustered into the shape of a heart, and was drizzled with red and pink glitter. Inside, she had written a poem to her parents. It was a very pretty card, but Kirsty couldn't help feeling that something was missing.

"I was hoping to add a little something else," she explained to Mr Brown. "Do you have any scraps of ribbon or paper left over from our project last week?"

"Oh yes," said Mr Brown with a smile. "You'll find what you're looking for in the cupboard in the hall."

Kirsty grinned and headed across the room and out of the door. Rachel followed just a few steps behind. "Wait, Kirsty!" she called, but her friend didn't hear.

Rachel stepped into the hallway just as

Kirsty opened the cupboard door. At once, a big box of art supplies fell on Kirsty's head – and two goblins tumbled out after it! Rachel noticed that one goblin was clutching a pink card with a sparkly red ribbon looped around it. The other goblin held a long, skinny wand.

As the goblins scrambled to their feet and dashed down the corridor, Rachel rushed forward to help her friend.

"My card!" Juliet cried, pointing from her perch on Rachel's shoulder. "That goblin has it!"

As Rachel lifted the box off Kirsty's head, colourful fabric, jars of glitter and paper scraps fell to the ground. "Are you OK?" she asked, worried.

"Yes – let's catch those goblins!" Kirsty cried.

As the girls ran down the hallway, Juliet peeked over Rachel's shoulder and twirled her wand. Magically, the box of art materials floated back into the cupboard with the paper and fabric scraps safely inside.

"The goblins are fast!" Rachel yelled, stumbling down the Village Hall stairs. The heavy main door scraped open when Kirsty pushed it.

The sky was growing dark as the sun set. The girls searched the paths outside for the

goblins, but they couldn't even hear any footsteps. It was almost like the goblins had simply disappeared!

"But they have my Valentine's Day card! What will we do now?" asked Juliet.

A Simple Swap

"Don't worry, Juliet," Rachel said. "We'll get your card back."

"That's right," agreed Kirsty, walking up to a large map outside the hall. "Maybe this will give us an idea of where the goblins went."

"It can give us more than an idea!" Juliet cried, flying off Rachel's shoulder.

"I think this map can tell us *exactly* where to find them." She straightened her skirt and lifted her wand.

"*Little hearts, be our guide, show us where the goblins hide.*" A cluster of heart sparkles burst out of Juliet's wand and whizzed straight to the map, landing on a place called the Playhouse Theatre.

"The theatre
is over there,"
Kirsty said,
pointing to
an old brick
building.
Juliet
immediately

flew towards the theatre. The girls ran
behind her, right up the front steps. The
carved wooden door creaked as Kirsty
pulled it open. At once, the three friends
could hear the two goblins' voices –
arguing! They were standing at the front
of the theatre on a small stage. Juliet and
the girls sneaked inside and peeked out
from behind the last row of red seats.

"Why did you mix up the message on
the card?" asked one of the goblins.

"Jack Frost told us to mix up all messages, especially Valentine's ones," the other goblin grumbled.

"Well, we can't read it now, so we don't know if it's real. We can't take it to Jack Frost like this!" The first goblin pouted. "It doesn't even have a sparkly red ribbon."

Juliet, Rachel and Kirsty looked at one another with wide eyes. The goblins didn't know that they had the real magical card!

Rachel leaned in to her friends and spoke as quietly as she could. "I think we would have spotted the ribbon if it had fallen off on the way here."

"So the ribbon is probably in the theatre," Kirsty mused. The girls peered over the chairs and peeked down the aisle, searching for the ribbon.

Juliet flitted into the
air for a fairy's-eye
view, being careful
to stay out of sight
of the goblins. With
a pretty twirl, she
swooped up and
down, in and out
of the rows of seats
until finally she flew
back down behind a row

at the front of the theatre. When the fairy
reappeared, the red ribbon trailed behind
her in the air.

Kirsty smiled broadly when Juliet
dropped the ribbon safely in her lap.
"Now we have the ribbon," she
whispered, "but we still don't have
the card."

"We have *a* card, though," Rachel said. "Perhaps we can trick the goblins into handing over the real card. Pass me the ribbon."

Kirsty gave the ribbon to Rachel.

"Now, can I have the card you made for your parents?"

Kirsty clenched the card tightly. Even during the mad dash to the theatre, she had managed to keep it crisp and clean.

"Oh, I don't want you to spoil it on my behalf…" Juliet began, watching Kirsty's face carefully. It was clear how much the card meant to Kirsty!

"It's OK," Kirsty said. "I trust Rachel." She handed the card over, and watched as her friend tied the red ribbon around it.

"Now, here's the plan," Rachel announced, her eyes sparkling. She

explained how they would trick the goblins. "Kirsty, follow my lead. And Juliet, don't let them know you're here!"

The two friends sneaked back to the entrance of the theatre, unseen. Then they stood up and pretended that they had just walked in. Juliet hid on Rachel's shoulder again.

"We're so lucky that we found the magic card," Rachel said loudly, trying to attract the goblins' attention. "Now we can just hide in this theatre until we know the goblins are gone."

Kirsty could hardly breathe. Out of the corner of her eye, she watched as the goblins on the stage listened to what Rachel had said. "Yes," she added. "Juliet will be so happy to have her card back."

"Oh no you don't!" shouted the goblin holding the wand.

"That card is ours!" the other goblin yelled. "Quick! Do a spell!" He nudged his goblin friend.

The first goblin pointed his wand at Kirsty's pretty card and chanted, "*Whatever leaves Fairyland and ends up lost, should always belong to Jack Frost.*"

"That's a silly spell," the other goblin scoffed. "It's too short! It won't work."

But suddenly the card floated out of Rachel's hand and zipped through the air towards the goblins.

"It's working!" they declared, jumping up and down with delight.

Juliet giggled as she kept her wand pointed at the card. It was Juliet's magic that was carrying the card to the goblins, not their spell. But the goblins thought they had snatched the magical card from the girls!

"No!" Rachel yelled. "I found it first!" She raced towards the stage, pretending to be very upset.

"It's ours," the first goblin said, holding the card tightly. "We get the pretty magic card. You can have this silly little one." He threw the real magic card at Rachel. Then both goblins chuckled meanly as they stumbled off the stage and ran out of the theatre.

Rachel picked up the card and carried it back down the aisle to Juliet.

"Thank you so much, Rachel," Juliet said. "Your plan worked perfectly. I can take my card back to Fairyland! Now families everywhere can enjoy Valentine's Day together."

With those words, Juliet waved her
wand and shrunk the card back to
Fairyland size. The message on the
front now read, *HAPPY
VALENTINE'S DAY!*

Kirsty couldn't help
smiling at their new
fairy friend. She was
thrilled that they
had helped Juliet get
her card back, but she
felt a little disappointed
that the goblins had taken her own card
in exchange. She'd just have to make
another one!

"Now we just have two of your
Valentine's objects to find!" Rachel said
with a smile. "Don't worry, Juliet. We'll
find them. No matter what it takes!"

Kirsty gave Juliet a big wave as the fairy disappeared in a beautiful burst of sparkly red hearts. Then Kirsty heard the honk of her family's car. She and Rachel ran outside to see Mr Tate pulling up in front of the Village Hall.

Kirsty smiled at her dad as she went to unlock the bikes. She was happy to see him, and even happier that she and Rachel had helped Juliet track down one of the missing Valentine's Day objects!

The Red Rose Romp

Contents

Morning Muffins

As soon as Kirsty woke up the next morning, she went to her desk. It was Valentine's Day!

"I have to make a new Valentine's card," she murmured, opening a drawer and searching for a clean sheet of paper. She glanced over at her best friend, Rachel Walker, who was still asleep on the camp bed.

Kirsty couldn't help thinking about the card she had made the day before. She was glad that they'd tricked the goblins into thinking that her card was Juliet the Valentine Fairy's magic card, but Kirsty still wished she could have given her own card to her parents. She had worked so hard on it!

Luckily, she remembered most of the poem she had made up for the card. She wrote it  on a new sheet of paper and drew some hearts on the page. It was simple, but it would have to do.

"Good morning," Rachel said, sitting up and stretching her arms over her head. "Happy Valentine's Day!"

"Same to you," Kirsty said, smiling. Rachel always woke up in a cheerful mood. It was one of Kirsty's favourite things about her best friend.

"We have a lot to do today," Rachel announced, getting up and sifting through her bag. "We should get going."

"First we need to have breakfast," said Kirsty.

"Of course," said Rachel, "although we mustn't take too long because we've got to help Juliet!"

Kirsty frowned at her, but then she remembered Juliet's warning. Since Jack Frost and his goblins had stolen Juliet's magical Valentine's objects, family, sweethearts, and friends everywhere weren't getting along. Even Rachel and Kirsty were affected, since they were best friends! They would have to make an extra effort to work together. Luckily, they'd been able to do that when they found the magic Valentine's card the day

before, and now family love had been
fixed.

"Maybe we should try to find the box
of chocolate hearts next," Kirsty offered.
If they found that object, then friendship
would be safe from Jack Frost's mean
spell – and Kirsty and Rachel's friendship
would be back to normal!

"That sounds good." Rachel pulled on a red-and-white striped shirt. "I just have to brush my teeth and call my parents to wish them a happy Valentine's Day. I'll meet you downstairs."

Kirsty went down into the kitchen. The smell of cinnamon was already wafting up the stairs.

When Rachel walked in to the kitchen a few minutes later, the room grew quiet. Mr and Mrs Tate both gave tight smiles. Rachel thought Kirsty looked relieved to see her.

"My mum made us heart-shaped muffins. Let's eat them on the way," Kirsty suggested quickly, gulping down her orange juice.

Rachel noticed that Kirsty's hands fumbled as she hurried to wrap the muffins

in a napkin. "Thanks, Mum. We'll see you later," Kirsty called over her shoulder as she rushed out of the room.

Rachel gave a confused wave and followed her friend. As soon as Rachel walked into the garage, Kirsty closed the door behind her. Kirsty's shoulders slumped as she let out a sigh. "My parents were fighting," she said.

"It was something silly about my mum not liking where my dad put the compost bin. But they both seemed really upset." Kirsty looked into her friend's eyes. "Do you think it's because of Jack Frost?"

"I'm sure it is," Rachel reassured her. "We really have to find the chocolate hearts *and* the red rose – friendship love and sweetheart love are both still in trouble."

It was funny – Kirsty didn't think of her parents as sweethearts, but she knew what Rachel meant. "Then we have to look

for the rose first. I don't like it when my parents argue," Kirsty said. "Especially on Valentine's Day."

Rachel paused. She had been hoping to look for the chocolate hearts first. She really wanted to make sure that friendships everywhere were safe! But instead of arguing, she made herself smile and said, "OK. Where should we start?"

The Florists

Kirsty led the way as the girls pedalled their bikes to the village square. They kept their eyes out for their new fairy friend. They hadn't seen Juliet since she'd taken the magic card back to Fairyland the day before!

Once they arrived in the village, Rachel and Kirsty locked up their bikes and sat on a bench to eat their muffins. "How are we going to track down that particular single red rose?" Rachel asked between bites. "Lots of people send flowers on Valentine's Day."

"My dad always uses that florist," Kirsty said. She pointed to a small shop down the street. It had an arched doorway covered in vines. The hand-painted sign in the window read FULL BLOOM FLOWERS.

Just then, the florist's van pulled up in front of the brick building. "Let's hope Juliet's flower hasn't been delivered to someone," said Rachel, brushing crumbs from her lap.

"There's only one way to find out," Kirsty declared. She stood up and headed towards the shop with Rachel close behind. Just as they reached it, a young man with short hair and glasses brushed past them. He stepped inside and the door started to swing shut right in front of the girls.

"Oh!" the man cried, catching the door just in time. "I'm sorry! I didn't mean to close the door on you. I was miles away!"

"It's OK," Rachel said. As she looked up at the man's face, she could see that his eyes were sad.

Rachel nudged Kirsty to make sure she noticed, too.

Inside the shop, a woman with short brown hair was arranging a display case of colourful flowers. "May I help you?" she asked. She held a pair of stem cutters in one hand. Her nametag read LILY .

"Yes," the young man said, stepping forward. "I need a red rose."

Kirsty and Rachel listened closely. They needed a red rose, too!

Lily bit her lip. "I'm sorry," she said, "but we don't have any red roses left. We haven't had them in stock all week.

Luckily, we haven't received very many orders – but that's very strange at this time of year!"

The man shook his head in disbelief. "You have to help me," he said, clutching

his hands together. "I tried to send red roses to my sweetheart, but black ones were delivered instead. The note on the card was mixed up, too. It wasn't what I wrote at all. Now she thinks I don't love her any more."

Rachel and Kirsty looked at each other with concern. This definitely sounded like the work of the goblins!

Lily took a deep breath. "Let me just see when we'll get more roses in," she said, turning to her computer. The keyboard clicked as her fingers tapped away. Then she looked up from the computer screen. "I'm very sorry, sir," she apologised. "I've been trying to order more roses from the local greenhouse all week, but the emails keep coming back all scrambled. And no one is answering the phone." Lily sighed. "Maybe you can take some bright, cheery tulips instead?"

"No, that won't do. I need a red rose," the man said sadly. "But thank you, anyway." His shoulders drooped as he turned and walked out the door.

"How awful!" Rachel said, turning to Kirsty.

Kirsty nodded. "It's also weird," she said. "Why wouldn't the greenhouse take orders for red roses on Valentine's Day? I think we need to visit Greenhouse Gardens on the other side of the village." She walked quickly towards the door.

Rachel didn't move, her brow creased with worry. She was still thinking about the man and his sweetheart.

"Come on!" Kirsty called from the doorway. At once, Rachel rushed to catch up with her friend.

Magical Mix-ups

Outside the florist, the girls hopped on their bikes. Kirsty zoomed out in front, leading the way. "There are really pretty gardens on the far side of Wetherbury," Kirsty yelled over the wind. "If anyone still has red roses, it's them."

Rachel nodded, pedalling hard to keep up with Kirsty. They left the village square and headed down a narrow road with tall trees lining both sides.

After a few minutes, something up ahead caught Rachel's eye. "Look at that sign!" she called to Kirsty. "What does it mean?"

Both girls slowed their bikes and examined the sign. "EGG SURE HARDEN NOSE," Kirsty murmured. "That's odd. I think I've seen this sign before, but with different words."

The sign was made of wood, and the letters were bright green. In each corner was a simple painting of a red rose.

EGG SURE HARDEN NOSE. As she read it, Rachel couldn't help but touch her nose to make sure it wasn't hard!

"It doesn't make any sense," she said. "They're real words, but it seems like they're all scrambled."

"That's it!" Kirsty cried. "I knew I'd seen this sign before. It's supposed to read GREENHOUSE GARDENS. The goblins must have been here! They used their wand to mix up the letters in the sign. We have to hurry – I bet the goblins are already at the gardens!"

Kirsty didn't look back as she tore down the road towards the gardens. In the back of her mind, she wondered if her parents

were still fighting. If she could just find
that rose, she would feel a lot better!

She turned down a gravel lane and saw
the first in a long line of buildings with
glass roofs. When she
noticed two gardeners
besides a fountain,
she squeezed her
brakes.

Kirsty glanced back
and saw Rachel far
down the lane. She
propped her bike
against a large tree
trunk. *I'll just ask some questions*, she
thought, striding along the cobblestone
path. The workers, who were both
wearing overalls and thick gloves, seemed
surprised to see her.

"Excuse me," she began. "Do you have any red rosebushes that are still blooming?"

The two gardeners looked at each other. "Yes, we still have whole greenhouses full of them," one said. "We hardly had any orders for red roses this year."

Kirsty couldn't believe her ears! Lily's emails from the flower shop must have been all jumbled by the time they reached the gardeners, thanks to the naughty goblins.

"But a group of kids just bought all the cut roses," the other gardener said. "It must be for some kind of school project."

"Yeah," the first gardener chimed in, "I saw them leaving the main building a few minutes ago. It looked like they all had green fingers and thumbs!" They both laughed.

Kirsty's eyes grew wide at the mention of green skin! "Thank you so much," she said, before racing back to her bike. Rachel was waiting for her there. "The gardeners said that some kids with green fingers and thumbs bought all the cut roses!" Kirsty exclaimed, swinging her leg over the bike seat. "It must be the goblins — let's go!"

"Kirsty," Rachel said happily, "look who's here." She smiled and pointed to her shoulder. It was Juliet! But the little fairy's head was lowered and her ankles were crossed. Her wand dangled loosely in her hand. She was clearly very sad.

"Cheer up, Juliet," said Kirsty. "You're just in time. We think we know where the goblins are!"

A Glum Fairy

Juliet looked up at Rachel. "Can you explain to Kirsty?" she asked in a tiny voice.

Rachel nodded and lifted her chin. "Juliet is sad because no one is enjoying Valentine's Day," Rachel began. "Not only that, but people aren't being good friends or working together."

Kirsty looked at her friend. She knew that Rachel was trying to make a point. "Are you saying that I'm not being a good friend because I rushed off ahead of you?" Kirsty asked indignantly. "But I was just trying to help!"

"But you could have waited for me," Rachel responded quietly. "We always track down the goblins together!"

Kirsty knew that what Rachel was saying was true. It was Jack Frost's magic again, making her act in a way that was out of character.

"I'm really sorry, Rachel," Kirsty said.

"That's better," said Juliet, flying up from Rachel's shoulder. "Now, let's

all work together!"

Kirsty nodded firmly.

Juliet swooped down between the girls. "Shall we shake on it?" she said, reaching her small hand out in front of her. Kirsty quickly placed a finger on top of Juliet's hand, and then Rachel put her finger on top of Kirsty's.

The fairy grinned. "*When best friends make a fairy pact, may their friendship stay intact,*" she said.

Kirsty waited for a burst of heart sparkles to leap from Juliet's wand, but nothing happened. "Was that magic?" she asked.

"Yes," Juliet replied. "The purest magic of all – true friendship." She smiled at

Rachel and Kirsty. "With the two of
you on my side, I know we can save
Valentine's Day!"

Rachel and Kirsty smiled at each other.

"Well, let's
go and find
the goblins!"
Rachel
declared.

"Let's go
through
this row of

greenhouses," suggested Kirsty.
"Maybe we can cut them off!" She
climbed on her bike and pedalled over the
bumpy cobblestone path, pausing to make
sure Rachel was right behind her.

As they came to a clearing, Kirsty
spotted the main building. She scanned the

paths for a sign of the goblins.

Juliet flitted off Rachel's shoulder and high into the air. After a quick search, she let out a cry.

"There! Just over that hill!" she said, pointing. Kirsty and Rachel took off at once. From the top of the hill, they could

see a band of goblins, all dressed like
farmers with checked shirts, dungarees,
and straw hats. Each goblin had a wagon
filled with buckets of red roses.

"If I didn't know who they were or
what they were up to, I'd say they looked
rather sweet," said Rachel, watching the
goblins pull the wagons down the steep,
dusty hill.

"But not when you remember that they
stole Juliet's rose!" Kirsty said.

"And that they want to take it back to
Jack Frost," Juliet added.

"Well, that's true. So let's get them!"
Rachel declared, thrusting her fist into
the air. All at once, she lost her balance
and fell onto the handlebars, and her bike
rolled forwards. A second later, Rachel
was speeding down the hill!

A Muddy Mess

"Help!" Rachel yelled as her bike sped towards the bottom of the hill – and the goblins. A cloud of dust rose into the air behind her.

"What's that?" one of the goblins screeched. "Watch out!"

Kirsty dropped her bike and ran after Rachel. Juliet flew right next to her. Kirsty's mind raced, trying to come up with a plan.

"Run for your lives!" yelled a goblin. "Get out of the way!"

The goblins started to scramble in every direction, their wagons slamming into one another.

Suddenly, the screech of brakes rang through the air. With a giant *crash*, wagons

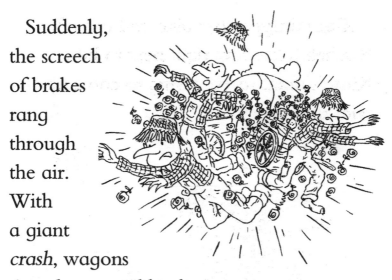

tipped over and buckets of roses spilled onto the path.

When the dust cleared, Kirsty was relieved to see that Rachel had landed in the soft grass. The goblins were not so lucky. They were in a muddy mess in the middle of the path!

"Something's pricking me!" one of the goblins screeched. "Yeouch!"

"Me, too," whined another goblin.

"Silly, thorny roses."

Rachel stood up and dusted off her knees. Juliet fluttered over to make sure that she wasn't hurt. Then she quickly

took shelter in the basket on the bike, so that the goblins wouldn't see her.

Rachel and Kirsty grinned at each other as they listened to the goblins whine and moan. "Oh, it hurts!" yelped another one.

Just then, Kirsty had an idea. "You poor

goblins," she said, kneeling down next to
them. "Do you need some help?"

"Oh, yes please. Get these horrible,
thorny roses off us!" they cried.

"Of course," Kirsty kindly agreed, gently pulling the roses away one by one.

When she came to the last goblin, Kirsty spotted something dangling from a rose's long stem: a sparkly red ribbon! Kirsty smiled with glee as she handed the rose to Rachel. Without a word, Rachel carried it over to Juliet in the bike basket. The goblins were all too busy moaning and grumbling to notice!

Kirsty pulled one last thorn off the goblin. "That's it," she announced.

"Hey, don't I know you?" the goblin asked, rubbing his side and peering at

Kirsty. "Wait! You're one of those pesky girls!"

"Pesky?" Kirsty questioned. "I just helped you and all of your friends. That doesn't seem very pesky to me." Kirsty put her hands on her hips.

"You weren't trying to steal Jack Frost's rose then?" the goblin asked, leaning so close to Kirsty's face that his long nose touched hers.

"Of course not!" Kirsty insisted. "I would never steal something that belonged to Jack Frost."

Kirsty chose her words carefully. She didn't want to tell a lie,

even to the goblins. But the rose didn't belong to Jack Frost. It belonged to Juliet!

The goblin squinted his eyes. "Fine, then. You can go."

Kirsty took a deep breath. She'd got the magic rose back, but she needed one more thing. "Could I have just one more rose? I'll let you choose which one I take." She bit her lip.

The goblin paused and then muttered, "Go ahead. Those roses are a pain, anyway."

He bent down and reached for a beautiful red rose that was in full bloom. He brushed a speck of dirt from one of the leaves and handed the rose to Kirsty.

"Thank you," Kirsty said sweetly, smiling at the goblin.

She walked over to Rachel and dropped the rose gently in the bike basket. Rachel wheeled the bike next to her, and the girls headed up the hill together before the goblins had time to notice that the magic rose had disappeared.

"Juliet has already gone back to Fairyland with her special rose," Rachel whispered. "She thought it was the safest thing to do. She said to tell you an extra-special thank you."

Kirsty smiled at her best friend. "Is it OK if we go back to the village square now?"

"Oh, yes," agreed Rachel. "We should tell Lily that there are plenty more red roses for the shop."

"And we know someone who wanted
just one single rose," said Kirsty, thinking
of the man who had visited the florist that
morning. As the girls looked at the rose
in the bike basket, magical red and pink
hearts swirled around the petals. When
they disappeared, the flower seemed to
glow. It was even more beautiful than

before. Sweetheart love was safe again!

"I can't wait to give this rose to him," Kirsty said. She grinned at Rachel. "I think it's going to be a very happy Valentine's Day after all!"

The Chocolate Heart Compromise

Contents

Loose Ends

"The magical red rose is definitely back in Fairyland by now," Rachel Walker said, glancing around the village square. "There are happy couples everywhere!"

Rachel's best friend, Kirsty Tate, nodded. It was the afternoon of Valentine's Day, and people were out walking their dogs and drinking coffee – two by two. Couples held hands and laughed. Sweetheart love was blooming all around Wetherbury!

"Now we just have one more Valentine's object to find," Kirsty said, watching as two workers put up a stage in the centre of the grassy square.

"The box of chocolate hearts," Rachel added. The final object was especially important to Kirsty and Rachel. After all,

the chocolate hearts maintained the love
between friends! Juliet the Valentine Fairy
needed to get the box of chocolate hearts
back to Fairyland as soon as possible.
It was the only way to make sure that
friendship love was safe from Jack Frost.

Kirsty and Rachel knew just how strong
Jack Frost's magic could be. Even though
they were best friends, they had been
arguing with each other a bit – and that
was most unlike them.

"Where do you think we should start
looking?" said Rachel.

"I don't know," said Kirsty. "But let's tie
up some loose ends and we might think
of something along the way. We should
go to Full Bloom Flowers first and talk to
Lily. We need to tell her that there are lots
more red roses at Greenhouse Gardens, if

she needs them."

"That's a good plan," Rachel agreed.

As the girls headed across the village square, Kirsty carefully carried the single red rose from Greenhouse Gardens. She could hardly wait to give it to the man whom they'd met earlier in the day.

When the friends entered the florist,
it seemed like a
different place.
The shop was
crowded with
customers, and
the phone
was ringing
nonstop. Lily
was wrapping
a large bouquet
behind the
counter. "Here
are your
daisies," she
said to an older
man wearing a
cap. "She'll love
them."

Kirsty and Rachel hurried to the counter.

"Excuse me," Kirsty said.

Lily looked up, and her jaw dropped. "A red rose," she whispered. "Where did you get it?"

"We just came from Greenhouse Gardens," Rachel told the florist. "They should have lots more roses to send your way."

"Really?" Lily questioned. "That's wonderful, but I haven't been able to reach the greenhouse by email or phone. It's been quite a worry!"

Rachel looked at Kirsty. How could they explain that those problems had disappeared as soon as Juliet returned the red rose to Fairyland? "Maybe you should give it one more try," Rachel suggested.

Lily looked first at her empty vases and then at all the customers in the shop. She reached for the phone and crossed her fingers. After a minute, Lily's eyebrows raised. "Gwen? I've been  trying to reach you all week!" She paused. "Absolutely! I'll take them all." Lily smiled as she hung up the phone. "Thank you so much!" she gushed to Rachel and Kirsty.

"No problem," Rachel said, smiling.

"Happy Valentine's Day!" Kirsty added.
They girls waved as they walked out of
the door.

The sun was bright, and Kirsty lifted one
hand to shield her eyes. In the other, she
still clutched the red rose.

"Oh! Look who's over there!" Rachel cried, pointing up ahead.

As Kirsty scanned the village square, she felt something slip through her fingers. Rachel had taken the rose! The next thing Kirsty knew, her friend was running across the street. Kirsty rushed after her, but by the time she reached the crossing, the light was red and she had to stop.

She watched Rachel stride towards a wooden bench – right up to the man with the glasses whom they'd seen in the flower shop earlier!

Best Friends Bicker

Kirsty bit her lip. She couldn't believe that Rachel had gone to see the man without her!

From across the street, she could see Rachel talking to him. His face lit up. He took the rose from Rachel and gave her a quick hug before rushing off, practically skipping across the square.

Just then, a flurry of fairy dust fell on Kirsty's nose. She looked up to see Juliet fluttering overhead. The tiny fairy darted to Kirsty's shoulder and ducked under her scarf. "Kirsty, I'm sorry," Juliet said softly. "I saw the whole thing. But you do know that Rachel didn't mean to hurt your feelings?"

Kirsty heard the fairy's kind voice and nodded, but she stil felt a bit upset. She suddenly realised that Jack Frost's magic must be even worse for other people. They didn't know that the goblins were mixing up messages, or that Jack Frost's spell was keeping friends from getting along. How horrible!

"We'll find the magic chocolate hearts. We can do it if we all work together," Juliet vowed.

The crossing light changed, and Kirsty set off across the street. Rachel ran to meet her.

"He was so excited!" Rachel exclaimed, clapping her hands. "He said it was the most beautiful rose ever. He couldn't wait to give it to his girlfriend. I wish you could have seen his face."

"Yes, I do, too," mumbled Kirsty, looking down.

"Oh," Rachel said, shrugging her shoulders. "I'm sorry you missed it."

Kirsty didn't want to argue with her friend. "Juliet's here," she said, changing the subject. Kirsty tilted her head so Juliet could peek out from beneath her scarf. The fairy gave Rachel a small smile.

"Hi, Juliet!" Rachel said brightly. "Sweetheart love is safe. Now we can focus on finding your last Valentine's object."

"Rachel?" Juliet's voice was quiet. "Did you know that Kirsty wanted to give the man the rose, too?"

Rachel paused. "I hadn't really thought about it," she admitted.

"I wish you had waited for me," Kirsty said, looking down at her shoes.

"You're right," said Rachel, reaching out to take Kirsty's hand. "I'm so sorry that I didn't think about you. Jack Frost's magic is getting to me! But let's work together to find the chocolate hearts now."

"OK," Kirsty said, feeling a little better. "How about we go to all the shops that sell chocolate? There's Poppy's Gifts, the Sweet Shop, and Mr Baxter's Market."

Suddenly, Juliet and the girls heard an awful screech. They turned to see two boys tugging at a scooter. There

was another yell as two girls nearby
fought over a pair of heart-shaped
sunglasses. In fact, when the three friends
glanced around, they saw groups of kids
quarrelling everywhere!

"All of those best friends are fighting,"
Juliet sighed.

"We have to find the chocolate hearts
right away!" Kirsty worried.

"Of course," said Rachel. "But let me
just pop to the loo first."

"OK," said Kirsty. "Why don't you
take Juliet with you for safekeeping.
She's less likely to be spotted and I can
stay on the lookout here. Let's meet by
the bikes."

Juliet flitted over to Rachel's shoulder
and waved as Kirsty headed towards
where she and Rachel had locked their

bikes.

Suddenly, Kirsty gasped. She searched for a pen and paper and quickly scrawled a note for Rachel:

THE GOBLINS
ARE HERE!
IN THE SQUARE!
WE'LL FIND THOSE CHOCOLATE
HEARTS YET!

When Rachel and Juliet came back just a few minutes later, Kirsty was nowhere to be seen. She wasn't by the bikes. They couldn't see their friend anywhere!

Another Mixed-up Message

"I thought she said to meet her by the bikes," said Rachel, peering around the square. "I hope she hasn't gone off on her own again."

"Look!" Juliet cried from her perch on Rachel's shoulder. "In the bike basket!"

Rachel reached into the straw basket and pulled out a piece of paper. When she unfolded it, she saw a note in Kirsty's handwriting.

I WILL FIND THE CHOCOLATE
HEARTS!
SEE THE TEAL QUEENS!
HEAR NO BERRY GHOST!

Rachel read the note again and again. The last two lines didn't make any sense, but the first line really upset her. "I can't believe that Kirsty would go to find the chocolate hearts by herself!" she said. "After everything that's happened."

"It does seem strange," said Juliet.

Rachel sighed. "I'm tired of bickering best friends and mixed-up messages," she muttered.

"Mixed-up messages!" Juliet gasped. "Let's read that note again!" Rachel held the paper up so Juliet could see it. "The last two lines make no sense," the little fairy said.

"It seems like they're scrambled," Rachel agreed. "Just like the sign to Greenhouse Gardens! So the first line is probably scrambled, too. Kirsty hasn't gone off on her own to look for the chocolate hearts at all!" She took a deep breath and looked around the square.

"But why would Kirsty have run off and only left a note?" Juliet wondered.

"Because of the goblins!" said Rachel.

Juliet followed Rachel's gaze to see a flash of green near the stage.

"They must have mixed up Kirsty's

note with their wand," Rachel guessed. "I think she wrote the note to warn us about the goblins. Then she had to hide from them."

"We have to find her," Juliet said. "And if the goblins are here, I'll bet the magical chocolate hearts are close by, too!"

Just then, a boy stepped onto the stage in the centre of the square. He looked about seven years old, and he seemed nervous. "Welcome to St Martin's School's Valentine's Day Show," he said. "Mrs King will lead the Year Two choir in song, and Mr Jones will direct the dancers."

A woman with curly hair led a group of children onto the stage. They walked in a long line and wore red and pink shirts. The audience clapped loudly. Next, a tall, thin man stepped onto the stage, followed by girls wearing white tops, wispy skirts, and ballet shoes. Finally, a group of boys dressed like Cupid appeared. After the graceful dancers, they seemed clumsy with

their big feet clomping on the stage.

"Hmmm," Juliet murmured. "Do they really need seven boys to play Cupid?"

"It's very strange," Rachel agreed. "And why are they...*green*?" Then she and Juliet looked a little closer. They burst into laughter. The boys dressed as Cupid were goblins!

Cupids and Chocolate

Rachel and Juliet watched the stage closely. The singers, dancers and goblins were all elbowing one another and frowning.

"No one is getting along!" Juliet sighed. Rachel turned and looked at the fairy perched on her shoulder. Juliet seemed tired…and sad.

Rachel and Juliet watched as Mr Jones, the dance teacher, tried to direct the show. The goblins were not only bumping into one another, but they even knocked over one of the ballet dancers!

Each time one of the goblins made a mistake, the others grumbled and scowled at him.

"Well, at least the audience thinks they're funny," Rachel said, watching the crowd laugh as the goblins tried to leap through the air while holding large hearts made of red card.

"Those Cupids are hilarious," said a man sitting in the back row.

"And at least the show is keeping the goblins out of the way," Juliet pointed out. "This is our chance to find Kirsty and the chocolate hearts!"

Rachel set off, jogging around the growing crowd. The choir began singing a ballad and the audience joined in.

Rachel passed the
bandstand and
then stopped to peek
around the back
corner of the
stage.

At once,
she saw
Kirsty.
Her best friend was
elbow-deep in large shopping bags
full of chocolate heart boxes.

Rachel was about to join Kirsty when
she saw something move on the far side
of the bandstand. The goblins!

"Kirsty," Rachel whispered loudly,
trying to alert her friend. "Kirsty!"

Kirsty looked up, delighted to see her.
She waved for Rachel to join her.

"Watch out!" Rachel yelled, pointing to the line of goblins coming around the back of the stage. Kirsty glanced over her shoulder and immediately straightened up.

She darted off behind an ice-cream van.

The best friends exchanged worried glances from afar as they watched the goblins scurry over to the bags of chocolate. "Come on, you slowcoaches!"

demanded a long-nosed goblin. "We have to hurry. The magic chocolate hearts are in here somewhere!"

"You're not the boss!" argued the goblin with extremely large feet. "We don't have to listen to you."

"Why is everyone whining?"cried the goblin who had given Kirsty the red rose at the gardens. "You're all annoying me even more than usual!"

Just then, Mr Jones appeared backstage. "Cupids, there you are," he announced. "The show is almost over. It's time to hand out the chocolate hearts to the audience."

"But we were just— " began the long-nosed goblin.

"No 'buts'," Mr Jones said. "Go and give those boxes of chocolate to the crowd! All of you."

The goblins glared at one another. They each picked up a bag and trudged off, grumbling all the way.

Goblin Goodies

Kirsty and Rachel watched the goblins approach the audience with the bags of chocolate hearts in tow. Both girls ran into the crowd, chasing different goblins, hoping to spot the box with the sparkly red ribbon. Juliet stayed hidden on Rachel's shoulder, so no one would spot her.

After a few minutes,
Kirsty spotted Rachel
across the square
and caught her
eye. Rachel
frowned and
shook her
head. Kirsty
did the same.
Neither
one of them
had found
the magic
chocolate yet!

Kirsty was
dizzy and
tired from
racing around
and scanning the crowd.

Then, out of the
corner of her eye,
she saw a flash of
green dashing
towards the
other side of
the square.
Kirsty raced
after it as
fast as she
could.
"Wait!"
she called.
"Please wait!
I need your
help!" Kirsty
was surprised
when the goblin
skidded to a stop.

"You need my help?"
the goblin asked.

Kirsty nodded,
recognising him as
the goblin who had
given her the rose.
He seemed to recognise
her, too. "I think you
have something I need."

As she said it, she peeked into the goblin's
bag and glimpsed a sparkle of red.

"But I need it, too," said the goblin.
"Why should I give it to you?"

"Well," Kirsty began, "the truth is, it's
not for me. I want to give it to my best
friend. Ever since the Valentine objects
went missing, we've been arguing. I hope
that if I give her the chocolate hearts,
things will go back to normal."

The goblin looked Kirsty in the eye. He reached into his bag and pulled out the box. The red ribbon shimmered in the afternoon sun. "Do you think these hearts will magically make you friends again?" he asked.

Kirsty paused. "We're still friends," she tried to explain. "But I think the hearts will help us remember how important our friendship is. Do you see how the hearts all have friendship phrases on them? This one says FRIENDS FOREVER, and this one says BEST FRIENDS."

The goblin bit his lip, and his chin trembled. Then, to Kirsty's surprise, he began to sob! "My friends and I have been fighting, too!" he cried. "I want to give them chocolate hearts. I want them to remember that we're best friends!"

Kirsty quickly searched her pockets and handed the goblin a tissue. He blew his nose, which blared like a trombone. She put her hand on the goblin's shoulder. "I think I can help you," she assured him. "Have a seat on this bench. I'll be right back."

Kirsty headed into the crowd again, searching for Rachel and Juliet. When she found them, she told them her plan. They all rushed back to the bench, and the goblin greeted them with a hopeful smile.

"Juliet has something for you," Kirsty said. With a whirl of her wand, Juliet created six small boxes of chocolate hearts. Each box was shaped like a heart! They gently floated down and landed on the bench next to the goblin.

"If you let us have Juliet's magical chocolate hearts, you can have these – there's a box for each of your friends," Rachel explained.

The goblin clutched the magical chocolate in his hands. He leaned over and looked at the chocolate hearts Juliet had made. "THE GOBLIN GANG," he read aloud from one piece of chocolate. "GREEN IS GREAT." A smile spread across his face. "It's a deal!" He hastily placed the magical chocolate hearts in Rachel's hands. "Your friend wanted to give these to you," he said. Then he gathered the six boxes in his arms and scurried off towards the stage.

Rachel, Kirsty and Juliet all cheered. "Soon all friends will be able to truly celebrate Valentine's Day, thanks to both

of you," Juliet said. When Rachel handed
the box with the sparkly red ribbon to
Juliet, it immediately shrank to fairy-size.
"Off I go!" Juliet exclaimed with
a wide grin. She gave both
girls a kiss and then
disappeared in a
twinkling of
heart-shaped sparkles.

Kirsty and Rachel both
let out big sighs of relief and
sank down on the park bench.

"I've never been so happy to see a
fairy return to Fairyland," Rachel said.

"It's hard to believe, but I think the
goblins are glad, too," Kirsty said. She
pointed across the square to where the
whole gang was sitting in a circle, reading
and eating chocolate hearts.

"And we can't forget all the happy sweethearts," Rachel said, pointing to a couple walking along, looking dreamily into each other's eyes.

"That's my parents!" Kirsty realised, a blush colouring her cheeks. Rachel giggled.

All at once, there was a burst of sparkles, and a red, heart-shaped velvet box appeared on the bench between the girls.

Rachel and Kirsty opened the box together. Inside was a handwritten note.

Thank you for being such good friends.
Happy Valentine's Day!
Love,
Juliet xx

Under the note, the girls found two
matching heart-shaped lockets which read
FAIRY FRIENDS FOREVER. They took turns

putting the
necklaces on
each other.
"They're
beautiful,"
Kirsty said.
"Yes,"

Rachel agreed, linking arms
with Kirsty. The girls were ready to share
the rest of Valentine's Day together – like
true best friends!

Win Rainbow Magic goodies!

There are seven hearts in
Juliet the Valentine Fairy and every one has
a secret letter in it. Find all seven letters and rearrange
them to make a special Fairyland word, then send it to
us. Each month we will put the entries into a draw and
select one winner to receive a Rainbow Magic Sparkly
T-shirt and Goody Bag!

Send your entry on a postcard to: Rainbow Magic
Juliet Competition, Orchard Books, 338 Euston Road,
London NW1 3BH.
Australian readers should write to:
Hachette Children's Books, Level 17/207 Kent Street,
Sydney, NSW 2000.

New Zealand readers should write to: Rainbow
Magic Competition, 4 Whetu Place, Mairangi Bay,
Auckland, NZ. Don't forget to include your name
and address. Only one entry per child.
Final draw: 30th January 2011.

Good luck!

Choose your own Magic

Have your own magical adventures with two favourite Rainbow Magic fairies!

Ruby the Red Fairy

978-1-40830-789-2

Katie and the Missing Kitten

978-1-40830-812-7

Look out for the Ocean Fairies!

ALLY THE DOLPHIN FAIRY
978-1-40830-815-8

AMELIE THE SEAL FAIRY
978-1-40830-816-5

PIA THE PENGUIN FAIRY
978-1-40830-817-2

TESS THE SEA
TURTLE FAIRY
978-1-40830-818-9

STEPHANIE THE
STARFISH FAIRY
978-1-40830-819-6

WHITNEY THE
WHALE FAIRY
978-1-40830-820-2

COURTNEY THE
CLOWNFISH FAIRY
978-1-40830-821-9

Available
April 2010